Josie and the Bad Hair Day

By Sharon Holt

Illustrated by Marjory Gardner

Chapter 1   A Decision   2

Chapter 2   Josh Goes Green   6

Chapter 3   Really Bad Hair   10

Chapter 1

A Decision

The bell had just rung, and there was a clatter of chairs as the children got ready to leave the classroom.

"Remember that tomorrow is Bad Hair Day at school," said the teacher. "I expect to see some colorful creations when you arrive tomorrow morning."

The room buzzed with excitement as everyone talked about their ideas for Bad Hair Day.

"I've decided to color my hair red," said Kylie.

"I'm going to put colored feathers in my hair," said Tommy.

Will talked about putting glitter through his hair. He asked Josh about his plans for Bad Hair Day, but Josh just shrugged his shoulders and wandered off without answering. He knew he would feel embarrassed with feathers or colors in his hair.

3

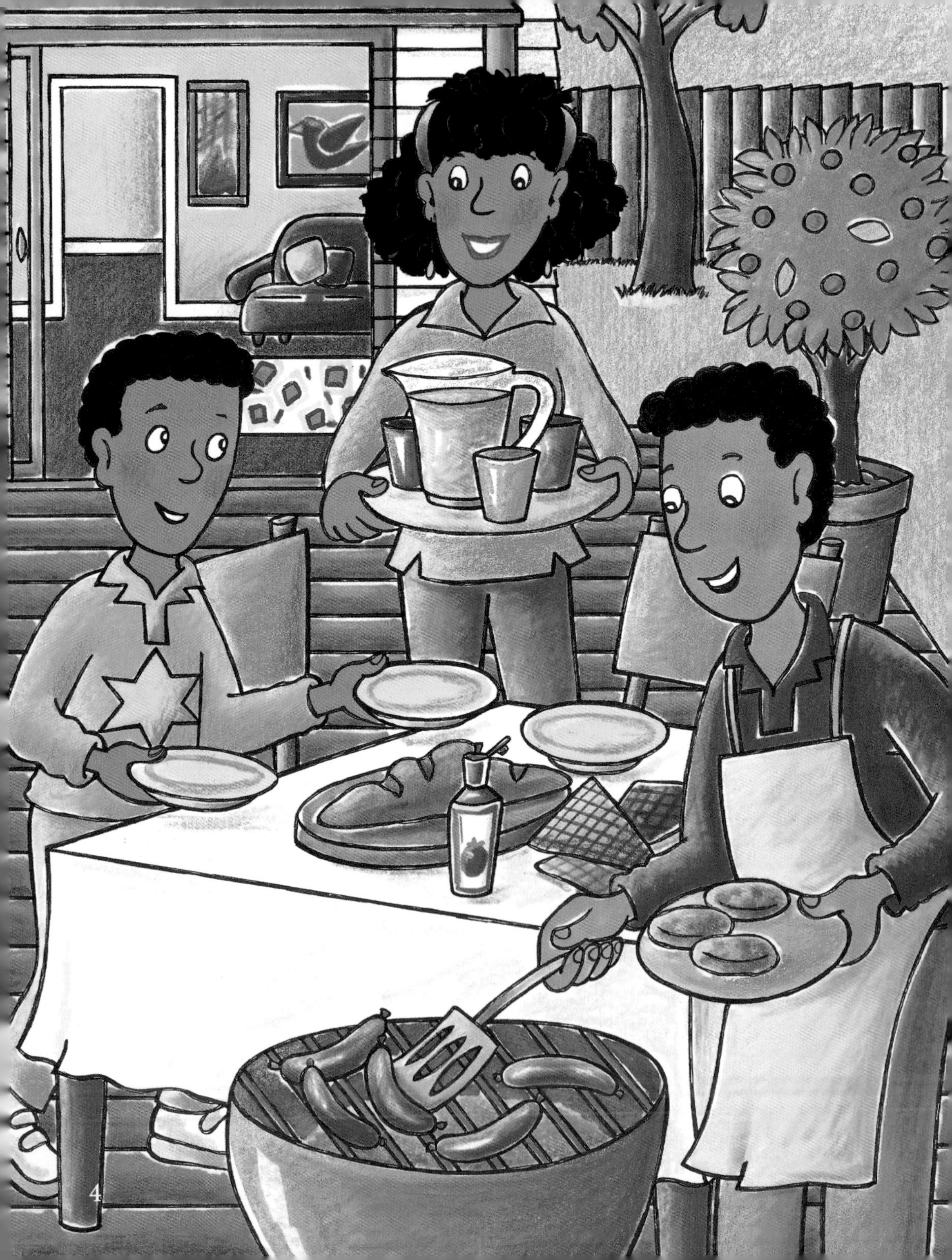

During dinner that night, Dad asked Josh about his day at school.

"Nothing much happened," Josh replied.

"I saw Will riding his bike when I arrived home from work," said Dad. "He told me about Bad Hair Day at school tomorrow."

Mom asked Josh about his plans for Bad Hair Day, but Josh said he didn't want anything different in his hair.

"I feel embarrassed when people laugh at me," said Josh.

"Nobody will laugh at you because everybody else will have bad hair, too," said Dad.

"Even the teachers will have something different in their hair," said Mom. "Are you sure you don't want to join in?"

Josh thought for a moment before answering.

"All right," he said. "You can put some hair dye in my hair in the morning, if you promise that nobody will laugh at me."

"I'm sure nobody will laugh," said Mom.

Chapter 2

Josh Goes Green

In the morning, Mom searched for the hair dye, but she couldn't find it anywhere.

"What about some food coloring instead?" she asked Josh.

Josh chose a bottle of green food coloring, and Mom spread it through his hair.

"Look in the mirror and see what you think," said Mom.

Josh looked at his reflection and saw a river of green running through his hair. He thought it looked quite good.

"The food coloring shouldn't take too long to dry," said Mom. "I suggest you keep away from water, and don't get too hot and sweaty or you'll be in trouble."

"Is it bad enough for Bad Hair Day?" asked Josh.

"I think so," said Mom. "We'd better hurry, or we'll never get to school on time."

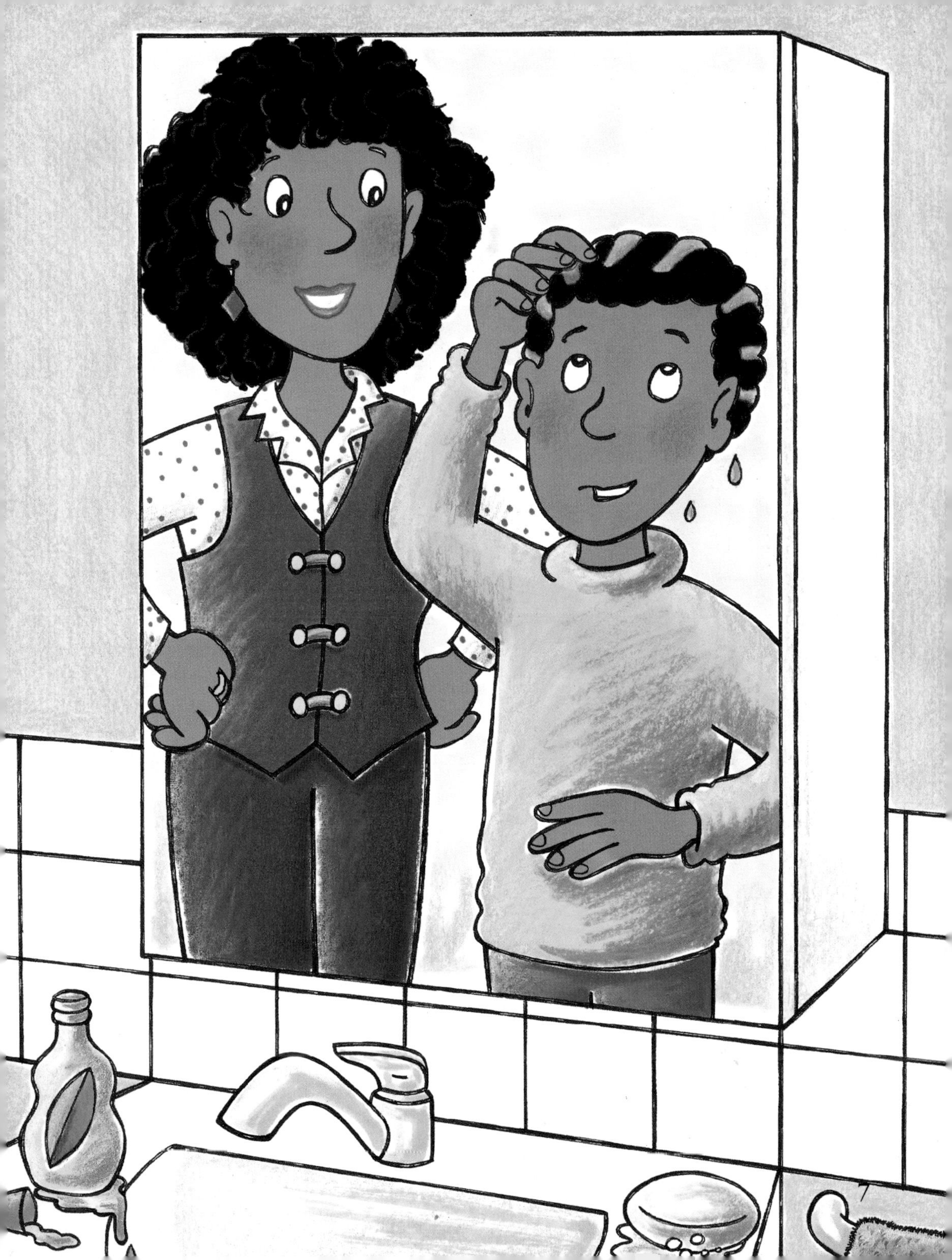

When he was getting out of the car, Josh noticed some splashes of green on his headrest.

“Never mind,” said Mom. “We can clean the seat later.”

When Josh walked toward the classroom, he saw that everyone’s hair looked different. Kylie’s hair was red with orange and yellow hair ties, and Tommy had colored feathers all through his hair. Josh noticed that several children had spiky hair, and his teacher’s head was covered with colorful clothespins.

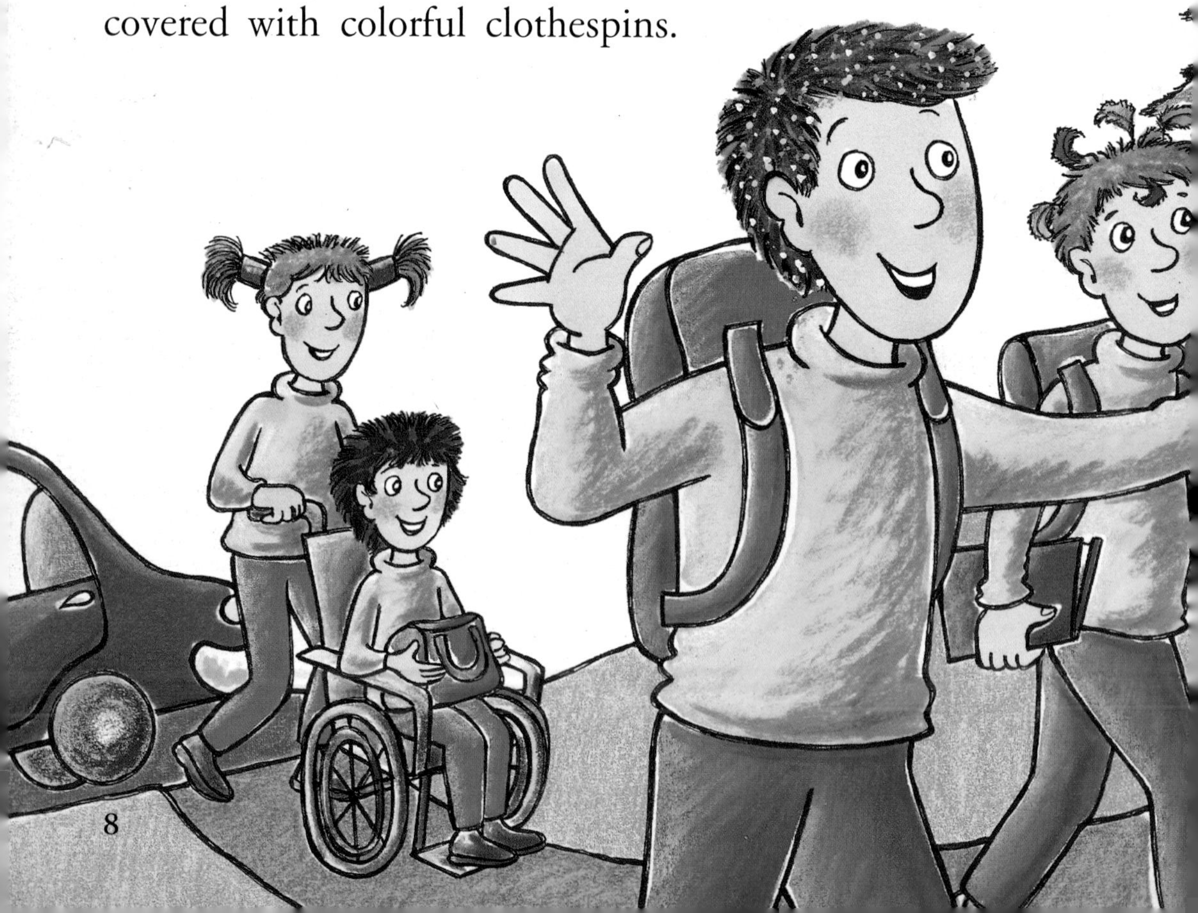

"Amazing!" said Will, staring at Josh's hair. "It looks just like green slime!"

"Thanks," said Josh, feeling proud.

Chapter 3

Really Bad Hair

In the classroom, the teacher had trouble settling the children down because they were so excited about Bad Hair Day. Some children were talking instead of working. Others were wandering around the classroom to get a closer look at everyone's hair.

Kylie groaned as she walked past Josh's chair. "Now I've got green slime marks on my sleeve because of your bad hair," she said.

"Sorry," said Josh. "The food coloring is still quite wet, but Mom said it should dry soon."

However the food coloring in Josh's hair took a lot longer to dry than he had expected. Tommy's head brushed past Josh's hair during reading time, and the teacher noticed a green mark above Tommy's eye.

"What's that green mark above your eye, Tommy?" she asked.

"It's nothing much," said Tommy, smiling. "Josh just slimed me with his bad hair."

At morning recess, a little girl came running up to Josh, pointing at the patches of green on the path behind him. "You're oozing slime!" she shouted.

"No, I'm not," said Josh, laughing. "It's just my bad hair."

When Josh washed his hands after lunch, some water splashed up onto his hair by mistake.

"Oh, no," he said to himself. "Now the food coloring is all wet again."

That afternoon green marks started to appear on his schoolbooks.

At the end of the day, the principal gave everybody certificates for coming to school with bad hair. When it was Josh's turn to get a certificate, the principal stopped and spoke to the whole school.

"There are no prizes on Bad Hair Day," she said, "but I think the certificate for the *worst* hair should go to someone whose hair has been really bad today!"

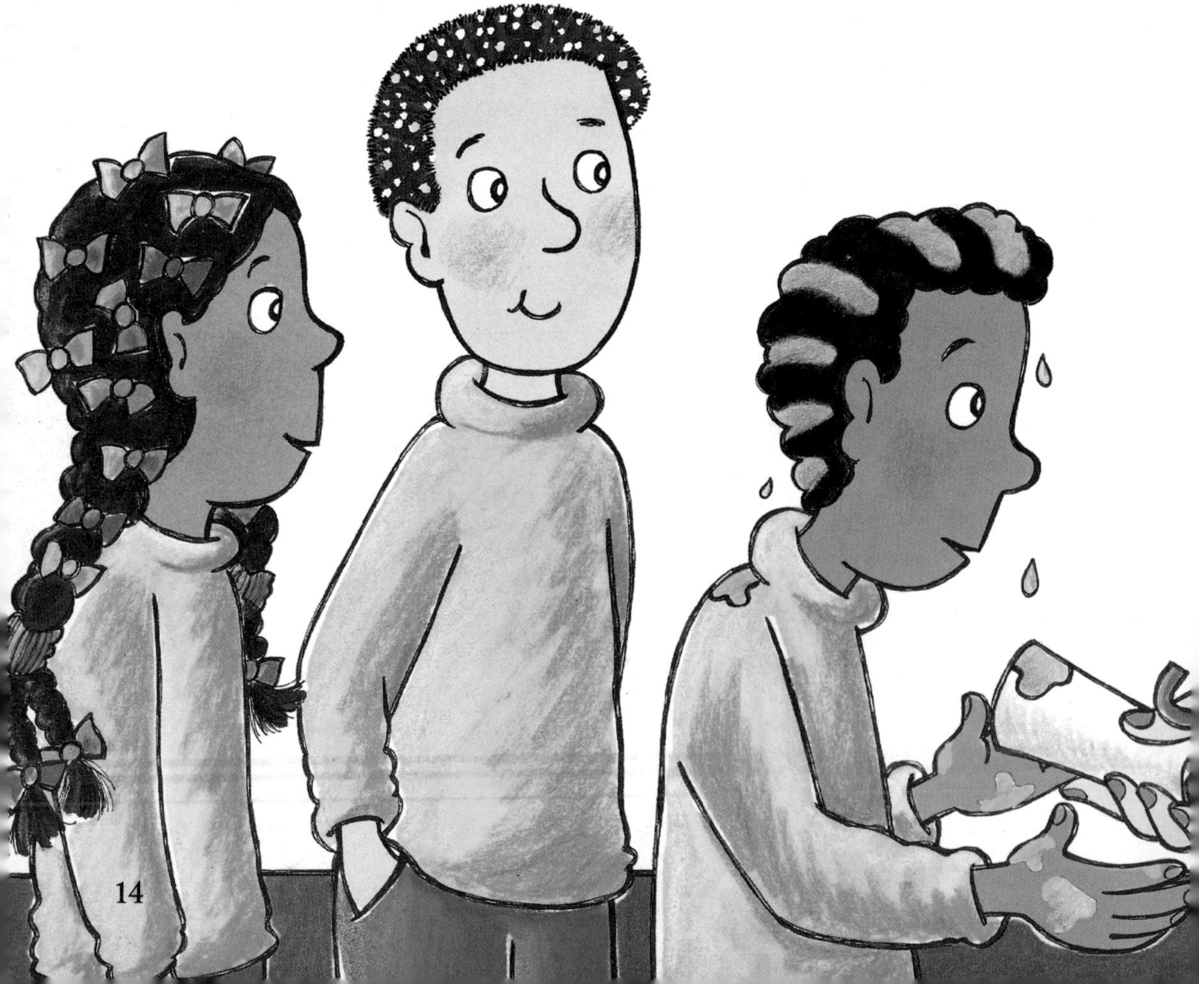

Everybody looked at Josh as he stared down at his green hands. He could feel his face getting hot and sweaty as the principal walked toward him. He kept looking down as she stood in front of him, holding out the certificate. Suddenly a splash of green fell from Josh's hair and landed on the corner of the certificate.

Josh looked up and grinned. The principal smiled back.

"I'm glad Bad Hair Day only comes around once a year, Josh," she said.

Everyone laughed – even Josh.